Happy Graduation!

Ms. Heather

To Mary M. Smith, the graduate
—M. M.

ALADDIN PAPERBACKS
An imprint of Simon & Schuster Children's Publishing Division
1230 Avenue of the Americas, New York, NY 10020
Text copyright © 2006 by Margaret McNamara
Illustrations copyright © 2006 by Mike Gordon
All rights reserved, including the right of reproduction in whole or in part in any form.
READY-TO-READ is a registered trademark of Simon & Schuster, Inc.
ALADDIN PAPERBACKS and colophon are trademarks of Simon & Schuster, Inc.

Designed by Sammy Yuen Jr.
The text of this book was set in CentSchBook BT.
Manufactured in the United States of America
First Aladdin Paperbacks edition June 2006
2   4   6   8   10   9   7   5   3   1
Library of Congress Cataloging-in-Publication Data

McNamara, Margaret.
Happy graduation! / by Margaret McNamara ; illustrated by Mike
Gordon.—1st Aladdin pbk. ed.
p. cm. — (Robin Hill School) (Ready-to-read)
Summary: The first graders in Mrs. Connor's
class prove that they can work together when Cookie
the dog disrupts their graduation ceremony.
ISBN-13: 978-1-4169-0509-7 (pbk.) ISBN-10: 1-4169-0509-X (pbk.)
ISBN-13: 978-1-4169-0510-3 (library ed.) ISBN-10: 1-4169-0510-3 (library ed.)
[1. Graduation (School)—Fiction. 2. Schools—Fiction.]
I. Gordon, Mike, ill. II. Title. III. Series.
PZ7.M47879343Hal 2006
[E]—dc22
2005030612

Robin Hill School

Happy Graduation!

Written by Margaret McNamara
Illustrated by Mike Gordon

Ready-to-Read
Aladdin
New York   London   Toronto   Sydney

Michael woke up early
on Graduation Day.
"Come on, Cookie," he said.
"You are done
with first grade too."

He put a cap
and a gown on Cookie.

"Now you are ready."

Michael took Cookie
to school.

He made sure she was safe.

In the classroom
Emma was fixing
Andrew's hat.

Hannah was tripping
on her gown.

Mrs. Connor took
the first-graders outside.

All the parents were there.

"Before I give out
the diplomas,"
said Mrs. Connor,
"I have something to say."

Woof! Woof!

"Woof, woof?" said Emma.

"Oh no!" said Ayanna.
"Cookie got loose!"
said Michael.

Cookie was running
all over.

She knocked over
the cupcakes.
She spilled the juice.

She grabbed a diploma
in her teeth.

"Come on!" said Becky.
The first-graders made
a circle around Cookie.

Kate called her name.
Nia held out a biscuit.

Michael picked up
her leash.

Emma rubbed her tummy.

"We saved the day!"
said James.

"Now line up!" said Becky.
And they did, perfectly.

"Well," said Mrs. Connor,
"I do not have to say
what I was going to say."

"Huh?" said Eigen.

Mrs. Connor said,
"I do not have to say
that you learned
how to listen

and how to work together."
She smiled.
"You *showed* that you
can do those things!"

The first-graders
got their diplomas.

The parents cheered
for all of them.

But Cookie got
the loudest cheer of all.